S0-BCL-597

For Sharon Cantor

K. L.

In memory of
EVERETT HAFNER,
my favorite
science fair bunny
M. H.

Text copyright © 2000 by Kathryn Lasky
Illustrations copyright © 2000 by Marylin Hafner

All rights reserved. No part of this book may be reproduced, transmitted,
or stored in an information retrieval system in any form or by any means,
graphic, electronic, or mechanical, including photocopying, taping,
and recording, without prior written permission from the publisher.

First paperback edition 2002

The Library of Congress has cataloged the hardcover edition as follows:

Science fair bunnies / Kathryn Lasky ; illustrated by Marylin Hafner. —1st ed.
Summary: In need of a replacement science fair project, two friends must
decide whether to use their loose teeth or leave them for the Tooth Fairy.
ISBN 0-7636-0729-0 (hardcover)
[1. Rabbits—Fiction. 2. Science projects—Fiction. 3. Tooth Fairy—Fiction.]
I. Hafner, Marylin, ill. II. Title.
PZ7.L3274 Sc   2000
[E]—dc21   99-046883

ISBN 0-7636-1735-0 (paperback)

10 9 8 7 6 5 4 3 2 1

Printed in Hong Kong

This book was typeset in Sabon.
The illustrations were done in watercolor and ink.

Candlewick Press
2067 Massachusetts Avenue
Cambridge, Massachusetts 02140

visit us at www.candlewick.com

SCIENCE FAIR BUNNIES

KATHRYN LASKY

ILLUSTRATED BY MARYLIN HAFNER

CANDLEWICK PRESS
CAMBRIDGE, MASSACHUSETTS

CLYDE WOKE UP AND GROANED.
"Oh, no! My bean plants wilted!"
"Not wilted, Clyde," his older brother Jefferson said. "They croaked. Dead. Dead, dead, dead."
"But those were for my Science Fair project," Clyde moaned.
"I'd say you're up a creek without a paddle. In big trouble. Down the tubes."

Clyde went to call his best friend.
"Rosemary?" he said. "I've got bad news. My bean
plants . . . they . . . died."

"Mine, too," said Rosemary. "What are we going
to do? The Science Fair is just a week away."
"I know," Clyde sighed.

"Why so glum?" Clyde's mother asked at breakfast.
"My Science Fair project . . . it's . . ." Clyde hesitated.
"A goner," said Jefferson.
"Oh, dear. Well, I'm sure you'll think of something,
Clyde. You're so clever," his mother said.

"Oh, brother," muttered Jefferson.

Clyde did not feel at all clever.

"You want to see clever?" Jefferson said. He got up and came back with a battery box, two wires, and a pickle. "Buster and I are illuminating pickles. Pickle juice is salty and it works like battery juice." Jefferson stuck a wire in each end of the pickle and connected the wires to the batteries.

"Ta da!" he exclaimed. The pickle glowed magnificently.

Clyde grew glummer and glummer.

"Eat your breakfast, Clyde," said his mother.

Clyde bit into his bagel. "Ouch! I forgot. I have a loose tooth."

"Is it ready to come out yet?" his father asked.

"No!" Clyde exclaimed.

He went to look at his new tooth. This was only the second tooth he had ever lost. The first had been bloody but at least the Tooth Fairy came.

He remembered how he'd wrapped the tooth in a piece of tissue all nice and lumpy and put it under his pillow with a note for the Tooth Fairy, and in the morning there was a shiny coin in its place.

Clyde pushed his tongue against the loose tooth. It moved a little.

Clyde pushed on his tooth all the way to school.
"What have you got in your mouth?" Rosemary
asked in science class.
"A loose tooth."

"Me, too," said Rosemary. "My first."

"Me, too," said Felix, as he and Phoebe set up a racetrack for their Wheels and Ways project with toy cars. "It's my third."

"My fourth," said Ralph, who was working on a weather chart with Abby. They had recorded the rainfall for the last thirty days. Clyde wished he and Rosemary had thought of a weather project. Weather was so dependable. It happened no matter what.

At dinner that night, Clyde's father said, "Let me look at that tooth."

"Promise not to pull it?" asked Clyde.

"I just want to see it," his father said. He looked into Clyde's mouth. "It's hanging by a thread."

"It's so glistening white," said his mother. "Like a little pearl."

Clyde thought of Granny McBunn. Her teeth were brown. His mother said it came from drinking so much tea.

Suddenly Clyde had an idea. "If I put my tooth in a jar of tea for a week, would it turn the color of Granny McBunn's?"

"Probably," said Clyde's father.

"Oh, Clyde, what a wonderful experiment! You're so clever!" said his mother.

"Oh, brother!" groaned Jefferson.

"But what about the Tooth Fairy?" asked Clyde.

"Well, Clyde," said Jefferson, "is it science or the Tooth Fairy?"

"Would it bleed if you pulled it, Dad?" asked Clyde.

"No," said Clyde's father. "Just one quick tweak."

"Okay, Dad. Pull it."

Clyde's mother poured hot water into a jar. Clyde put in a tea bag. He dropped in his tooth and went to the telephone.

"Rosemary, how's your tooth?"

"Hanging by a thread," she said.

Then Clyde told Rosemary what he'd done. His tooth was in tea and she could put hers in orange Jell-O.

"It's a really good experiment," he said.

"But what about the Tooth Fairy?" Rosemary asked.

"I don't know."

"I've got to think about this, Clyde. It's my first tooth, after all," said Rosemary.

That night, when Clyde's mother tucked him in,
she told him again how clever he was.

"That's the third time," Jefferson muttered.

When Clyde fell asleep he had a dream about the Tooth Fairy. He was in a laboratory. There were jars and jars of teeth in different liquids—tea, milk, orange juice, grape juice, lemonade, soda pop—all turning strange colors. The Tooth Fairy was wandering around, looking confused. "I just don't understand, Clyde. How could you do this to me?"

"Science," said Clyde. "We did it for science."

He was about to explain how the beans had died when his mother woke him up for school. "Look, Clyde, your tooth is darker!"

Clyde blinked. The tooth *did* look different!

He got out his paper and colored pencils and drew a picture and labeled it. Mr. Bunson, his science teacher, said that record keeping was part of good science. He called it "data."

On his way to school, Clyde wondered what Rosemary had decided. A one-tooth experiment wasn't much. He needed a second tooth at least. He ran his tongue around his mouth. Nothing was loose. Clyde began to despair.

When he got to school, Rosemary rushed up to him. "Strawberry!" she cried.

"Strawberry what?" asked Clyde.

"We only had strawberry Jell-O." Rosemary smiled. There was a big gap where the tooth had been.

"Rosemary! You did it!"

"It was for science, Clyde. Now we need more teeth."

They put up a sign and waited for people to give them teeth. Finally Claudia and Daphne came by.

"Daphne and I lost our teeth this morning," Claudia said. "You can have Daphne's. The Tooth Fairy will give us double the money. It works that way when you're twins."

"That's great!" said Rosemary.

Grape juice! Clyde thought. *We'll put Daphne's tooth in grape juice.*

All week long Rosemary and Clyde soaked the three teeth. Every day they made notes and drew pictures as the teeth in the jars darkened. On the day of the Science Fair, Rosemary's father drove them to school with their posters and a carton with the three jars of teeth.

"Good luck!" Clyde's mother called.

The Science Fair
projects were set up
in the auditorium.
Albert had done an
experiment with
bacteria that ate
oil slicks.

Harry and Edward
had done one called
Potions and Explosions,
with baking soda and
vinegar.

"Wow, Rosemary!"
exclaimed Clyde. "Look
at that bacteria experiment!"
Rosemary made a face.
"His parents did it. You can tell."
"Well, I guess no one
could say that about ours."
Clyde sighed.

The judges were coming. "My goodness," said one judge, "you made a sign asking your classmates to donate their loose teeth and only one did?"

"Right." Rosemary nodded.

"It was the Tooth Fairy," explained Clyde. "They didn't want to disappoint the Tooth Fairy."

"See, we wrote it right there."
"Yes, I see," said another judge. "Very interesting."
The judges made notes and then moved on.
Clyde and Rosemary waited nervously.

Soon it was time for the announcement of the Science Fair awards.

"The award for best presentation of facts goes to Felix and Phoebe for their Wheels and Ways Experiment," said the principal. Everyone applauded.

"The blue ribbon for best scientific procedure goes to Susan, Betty, and Mickey for their Kitchen Crystals Experiment comparing the abilities of sugar-based mixtures to form crystals." More applause.

YOU HAVEN'T GOT A CHANCE!

"And finally the blue ribbon for the project that demonstrates the most original and independent work in the entire Science Fair goes to Clyde and Rosemary for their Yucky Teeth Experiment."

"I can't believe it! We did it! We did it!" yelled
Rosemary and Clyde, jumping up and down.

"You thought of the idea, Clyde."

"Well, it was just that my tooth was loose. And
you gave up your very *first* tooth, Rosemary."

"It was for science," she said.

"I guess so," said Clyde. "I hope the Tooth Fairy
understands."

The next morning when Clyde woke up he felt
something under his pillow.
It was a nice, lumpy little package.

He unwrapped the tissue. A shiny coin glittered,
and beside it there was a tea-colored tooth.
There was a note, too.

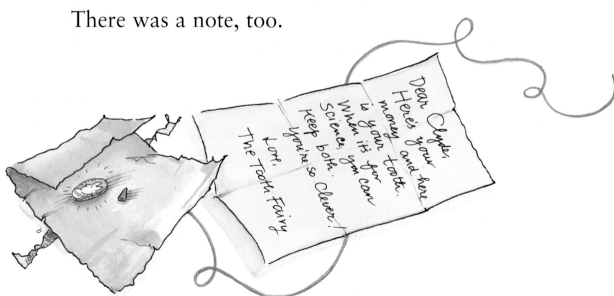

Dear Clyde,
Here's your
money and here
is your tooth.
When it's for
Science, you can
keep both.
You're so clever!
Love,
The Tooth Fairy

"Hey!" said Jefferson. "Come look at my new pickle flashlight. Want me to wire up that tooth for you and make it glow?"

"No thanks. I think I'll just keep it the way it is."

"For science?" Jefferson asked.

"No, just to remember."

And then Clyde went to call Rosemary
to make sure that she kept her tooth, too—

just to remember.